HALLOWEEN AT THE BAKER VALLEY BARKERY & CAFE

ALSO BY ALEKSA BAXTER

MAGGIE MAY AND MISS FANCYPANTS MYSTERIES

A DEAD MAN AND DOGGIE DELIGHTS

A CRAZY CAT LADY AND CANINE CRUNCHIES

A BURIED BODY AND BARKERY BITES

A MISSING MOM AND MUTT MUNCHIES

A SABOTAGED CELEBRATION AND SALMON SNAPS

A POISONED PAST AND PUPPERMINTS

A FOULED-UP FOURTH

A SALACIOUS SCANDAL AND STEAK SIZZLERS

NOSY NEWFIE HOLIDAY SHORTS

HALLOWEEN AT THE BAKER VALLEY BARKERY & CAFE

A HOUSEBOUND HOLIDAY

HALLOWEEN
AT THE
BAKER VALLEY BARKERY & CAFE

A NOSY NEWFIE HOLIDAY SHORT

ALEKSA BAXTER

ISBN: 978-1-950902-64-4

CHAPTER 1

It was early afternoon on a gorgeous late fall day in the Colorado mountains. Fancy—my three-year-old Newfoundland—was sound asleep in her cubby behind the barkery counter (you read that right, barkery, as in bakery for dogs), her legs thrust towards the ceiling as she happily snored away.

I was all alone. It was Jamie's day off and our shop assistant had already left for the day. I wasn't expecting any more customers, so I cranked the music up as I wiped down the tables and belted out how there's no one like me right along with Taylor Swift.

I can't sing to save my life, but I honestly, truly did not care. Just like I didn't care that I was cleaning—something I normally hate to do. Because, well, I was hopelessly, pathetically in love. It was a horrible feeling, all giddy and gooey and happy. But in that moment, filled to the brim with thoughts of Matt, a/k/a Officer Handsome Distraction a/k/a *Mine*, I didn't care that I was infected with some sort of brain-eating insanity that stole all my self-respect.

All I cared about was the fact that I, bitter, jaded, crazy person that I was had found a boyfriend that I really, really liked. That thought alone made me crinkle my nose, smile, and add an extra little bootie shake as I wiped down the last table in the corner, my blonde braid whipping back and forth as I really got into it.

Life was good. Life was *very* good.

Sure, there were some changes coming, including the fact that we were going to have to close down the barkery soon so that it could be replaced with a top-notch luxury pet resort catering to not only dogs but cats and probably geckos, too. But that was okay.

I was almost excited about it. Me and luxury don't exactly go hand in hand, so that scared me some. But I'd still get to run a business with my best friend, Jamie. And with her fiancé Mason and with Greta, my newest friend and a woman who had one of the most colorful pasts I've ever encountered.

Also…And this was maybe the best of all. I'd get to keep designing fun new dog treats but I wouldn't have to work the counter and be "on" all the time.

Not that I'd been having a problem with that lately, because I had a boyfriend (!) and it made me all giddy, happy, friendly. It was a very odd feeling. Like an out of body experience, really. But that had to end at some point. You can't stay on a love high forever.

Which meant eventually I'd be very happy for that pet resort and my new role as Chief Treat Developer even if it would probably be best for the business to keep me locked away in a dark backroom somewhere.

But that was in the future.

In the present it was time to work on my plans for the first (and only) Halloween Pet Parade at the Baker Valley Barkery and Café. I figured if we were tearing the place down we should go out with a bang. So our last day of business was going to be the Saturday before Halloween and we were going to have a big, huge costume party for pets and people.

Which meant figuring out what to make Fancy.

Not the easiest of tasks. You see all these dogs in these cute little costumes and you think, "Oh, I love that. I could totally do that with my dog." And then you try it on your hundred-and-forty-pound dog and it doesn't really turn out so well.

I once bought Fancy those little snow booties to protect her feet when she was a puppy because we lived in an apartment and they put that awful deicer stuff all over the sidewalks and I didn't want her to get it on her paws. Yeah, that lasted about five minutes.

She tore one off with her mouth, kept shaking her feet to get the front ones off, and wouldn't even let me near her to get the fourth one on, all the time giving me one of those looks that asked "Why would you do this to me? What have I done to deserve this sort of torture?"

So nothing on the feet. Which ruled out the cute little bowtie and cuff set I'd found.

The Halloween before I'd tried one of those bee costumes on her, the type that come with a little hat and wings that attach around the back. She was okay with it for a minute or two—long enough to get a cute picture. But then…

No.

She kept spinning in circles trying to get the wings off her back. And clawing at her head to remove the hat. It took all I had to get her calmed down enough to get the outfit off of her.

And don't even get me started on the Santa hat…

Of course, it did make noises and turn psychedelic colors if you pushed the little white ball at the tip so I really can't blame her on that one. She did actually tolerate it. She just looked so miserable the whole time I felt like the worst dog parent on the planet.

It seemed I'd have to get my fill of clever dog costumes from my clientele.

But I so wanted to make Fancy into a loofa. Or an Energizer Bunny. Or a teddy bear. Or a panda.

(I really wanted to make her a panda…)

Seriously, I needed to stay off Pinterest.

But they had such cute pictures. It made me want to have like ten Newfoundlands instead of one. And then I could dress them all up for a Mad Hatter-style tea party with funky little hats and giant-sized tea cups with dog biscuits on little colorful plates and…

Yeah, I know. I was losing it. Love, I tell ya. Fries the circuits.

But, hey, at least I wasn't as bad as the woman I knew who dressed her dogs up as a bride and groom and had them get married. Not that there's anything wrong with that if you yourself have done so. Not even if you sent out embossed invitations, hired the best caterer in the county, and had a swing band perform at the reception.

You are perfectly normal. No one is judging you. Really. Truly. I swear.

(Okay, so I'm not a good liar. Whatever.)

Anyway. I needed to figure out a costume for Fancy. But first I wanted to figure out a new treat to give out at the party, because of course a pet Halloween party has to have trick or treating.

We already had our staples: Doggie Delights, Canine Crunchies, Barkery Bites, and Mutt Munchies. (I still winced every time I said that last one, but it was what it was and they did actually sell well—to my surprise and amazement.)

But I wanted something new for the party. We were going to keep the online store open during construction and the party would be a perfect opportunity to get some fun photos for the website and introduce a new product.

I figured it should be Halloween-themed, though. Which meant finding an appropriate name. Maybe Ghostly…something.

Or Devilish…Delights. No, I'd already used delights. Devilish Delishes? No. That didn't work. Too much sh-ing.

But maybe Boolicious…?

Bites?

Or Booberry Bites?

Or Boolicious Booberry Bites? That was a mouthful.

And it used bites again which I'd already used for Barkery Bites.

I frowned out the window, trying to work it out. Boolicious, Booberry, ba, ba, ba, ba, ba. I found myself tapping my foot along with the sound and made myself stop.

And then I had it.

Booberry Biscuits. *That* would work. A little bit of blueberries, maybe some banana…Yeah, that would definitely work.

I did another little bootie shake and headed for the kitchen. Time to create a treat that would live up to its boolicious name.

CHAPTER 2

Fancy was definitely a fan of the end product. Then again, Fancy would probably eat saw dust on the off chance it was tasty so perhaps she's not the best judge of quality. Although she has declined to eat cauliflower, so she does have some standards. Albeit low ones.

Because I'd wanted to finish baking the last batch of biscuits, I was running late when I finally left the barkery. Not that traffic was bad.

That was one of the best perks of living in the Colorado mountains. No real traffic to speak off. I mean if we'd lived along I-70 we'd have been faced with some crazy tourist traffic where people drive like they're in some sort of speed-based death race weaving in and out of large semis hauling produce cross-country, but we didn't.

We were on one of those highways that shoot off of I-70 and are considered a scenic byway, so things were a lot more relaxed and calm. Even though it was technically a highway it was only one lane going in each direction so the real insane drivers who had to get somewhere fast stayed away—get stuck behind a cattle truck and a double-yellow line once and you learn your lesson.

So the twenty-minute drive from the barkery to my grandpa's place in Creek was beautiful and relaxing. The whole valley was surrounded by mountains and capped with a blue sky covered with filmy clouds that were colored pink and purple as the sun set.

Heaven.

Absolute heaven. And so far removed from my old life in DC it was hard to think about. But I'd made my choice. And I was…happy with it. Nervous. More nervous than I'd been about anything in my life, ever. Probably because this was the first time I'd decided to stay somewhere instead of moving on to the next, best choice. It's surprisingly hard to say, "Yeah, this is what I want" when your nature is to explore and try new things.

But it *was* what I wanted. I had Fancy. I had my grandpa. I had time with my best friend. I had Matt, which made me smile to myself and then blush even though no one was around to see it.

I had it all. For now. Which is all anyone can ever hope for.

Of course, when I finally walked in the front door and my grandpa gave me "that look" I was reminded that no matter how perfect life is it's never actually perfect.

"Maggie May…"

"Sorry I'm late. I really am. I got caught up making a new treat for the party." I kissed him on the cheek as he grumbled at me. He was my rock. In his faded jeans and flannel shirt—long-sleeved now in honor of the changing seasons—his hair still a light brown despite his eighty-plus years.

He patted my arm. "Don't tell me. Tell Lesley."

I made my way towards the kitchen and the smells of some delicious concoction I couldn't identify. "Hey, Lesley. How are you? Sorry I'm late."

Lesley, my grandpa's friend who was probably now his girlfriend but that was just too weird a term to use for two people in their eighties, was at the stove, stirring some sort of sauce that bubbled with the scents of red wine and mushrooms.

She looked as polished as ever with her white hair pulled back from her face and her impeccable makeup. The only concession she'd made to cooking was to remove her jewelry and leave the rings and bracelets in a small pile on the kitchen table. She had an apron tied around her narrow waist, and if I wasn't mistaken the cute little coffee cups dancing along the edge were cross-stitched by hand.

"It's okay, Maggie. Matt called to say he was running late, too, so we're probably ten minutes from dinner being ready."

"It smells delicious." I leaned in for a deeper whiff, but Lesley's flinty look told me not to try for a taste.

I'm not a bad cook. I can make a Crockpot recipe or a simple casserole with the best of them, but what Lesley had done in that kitchen was a whole level of sophistication above anything I can pull off. There were crisped potatoes with real fresh herbs of some sort and that wine sauce along with some form of beef that looked tender enough to melt at the first bite.

I sniffed the air.

"Is that an apple pie?"

She nodded.

"I tell ya, Lesley, if we weren't demolishing the café and barkery I'd argue for hiring you to come run the place."

She laughed. "Oh, I'd never want that. Retirement is good for me." She smiled at my grandpa who was standing in the doorway.

When he smiled back at her I suddenly felt like the odd one out. "Well, then. I think I'll sneak off to change real quick if that's okay with both of you."

They didn't even notice as I raced out of the kitchen before they did something crazy like kiss. I no longer begrudged my grandpa his relationship with Lesley—I'd come to see that he deserved to move on now that my grandma was gone and that Lesley was a great fit for him—but I still had that childhood cooties reaction to the thought of anyone older than me kissing or…well, let's leave it at kissing.

And I did need to change. When I get to baking it's a mess. I don't know why I find it so hard to run a blender and not kick up flour in every direction, but I do. I'd also somehow managed to sit in the batter. How had I done that? When had I done that?

I'd just finished throwing on a new pair of jeans and a different t-shirt when someone knocked on my bedroom door. I opened it to see Matt standing there and just sighed in pleasure.

He's a great man. Solid as a rock. Kind. Funny. Intelligent. But he's also darned fine looking. All tall and lean with these great blue eyes and dark hair and that smile and…

Alright, enough. I know how annoying people in love can be, because I'm not usually one of them so I have to suffer through it a lot myself. But he is very attractive. And he was mine. And he was standing there in the doorway and my grandpa and Lesley were off in the kitchen somewhere.

So I kissed him.

Which just made me smile all that much more. Seriously, they really need a cure for that stuff. It's just not healthy to live like that.

CHAPTER 3

At dinner I told everyone about my dilemma trying to figure out what to make Fancy that she'd actually wear at the party.

"Honestly," I said as I took another bite of the most delicious meal I'd ever eaten in my life, "the only thing Fancy has ever worn without complaint was a doggie GoPro I got her when she was about a year old."

"What's that?" my grandpa asked.

"A GoPro is a camera that a lot of athletes use. I used to know a bunch of skydivers who used them to film their jumps. They're small and pretty tough so good in situations like that. Mountain bikers like to use them, too. Anyway. Turns out they sell a harness that dogs can wear so you can strap a camera to your dog's chest or their back and see the world from their viewpoint."

My grandpa took his time finishing his last bite of food. "Let me get this straight. You spent good money to buy a camera that you strapped to your dog so you could see how things looked from her perspective?"

"Mmhm. I actually had this whole idea where I'd take Fancy to different dog parks in the area and have her wear the GoPro and capture footage of the place and then I'd start a website where I rated each dog park and had a video for each one that was partially footage from me and partially footage from Fancy. I actually wanted a friend of mine with a little dog to come along so we'd have the big dog perspective and the little dog perspective and they could see each other in the footage and..."

I stopped talking because my grandpa was just looking at me like I'd lost my mind.

"What? It could've totally worked. Fancy is adorable. People would absolutely watch a show that involved her."

"You think so. You think people have nothing better to do with their time than watch your dog go to dog parks?"

"You'd be surprised, Grandpa. But I didn't know enough about filmmaking to pull it off. The footage was so bumpy it made me nauseous just to watch it. I'm sure there's some way to fix it, but I never bothered to find out what."

Matt dropped a piece of potato on Fancy's plate where she sprawled on the floor between the two of us. "You know...You could have her wear the GoPro that day."

"And?"

"Maybe that's all you need. Put a pad of paper and a pencil on her harness or something and call her an intrepid reporter."

"Well, Peter Nielsen is a dog, that's for sure." (He was the local reporter for *The Baker Valley Gazette* and had tried to ruin my business with a few unwarranted smear articles that I hadn't appreciated one little bit.)

I pouted. "But I wanted to make her a panda. Wouldn't she make an adorable panda? I could put white pajamas on her and leave her feet bare and then a little white hoodie with her ears poking out of the corners and her nose in the middle?"

Matt just looked at me. "You could certainly try that."

"But it won't work, will it?"

Fancy watched us both with attentive interest but I knew that was more out of a desire for another bite of food than any actual understanding of what we were discussing. I looked down at her and frowned. "You'd never let me do it, would you? As much of a slug bug as you are, why won't you let me dress you in silly costumes?"

She raised one eyebrow at me in that way she has.

"I know. Dignity. It's the same reason I never trained you to do tricks. If only I'd started on you when you were young..."

Fancy harrumphed and put her head on her paws, still watching me out of the corner of her eye for another bite of food. I snuck her a green bean as I turned back to the conversation.

"Intrepid reporter, huh?"

Matt nodded. "And it will give you video footage of the event. You might even be able to use it for the website if we can find someone to solve that shaking issue for you."

"Okay. Fine. It's a good idea. And possible, which is most important of all."

My grandpa smiled at both of us. "Now, the real question. What are you two going to wear?"

I stared at him in horror. "Nothing. It's a pet party, not a human party."

Matt cleared his throat. "I happen to know that Jamie and Mason are going to wear costumes."

"Oh no. Don't tell me that. Jamie loves wearing costumes. What is she coming as?"

"I can't say. I'm sworn to secrecy."

I glared at him, but when he makes a promise he keeps it. "Just because they are, doesn't mean we have to."

"It'll be fun." He leaned back in his chair. "I was thinking you and I could go as Elvis and Marilynn Monroe?"

I laughed. "No."

"You'd make a great Marilynn."

"No, I would not, but that's very sweet of you to say. I usually just put my hair in two braids, wear some peace symbol jewelry and a long dress, and call myself a hippie."

"That's no fun. Come on, we have to be creative about this."

"We?"

"Well, now that we're a couple we should match."

"We should?" I squeaked.

I tried to hide it but the thought of being one of those people who dresses up in matching costumes with my boyfriend made me want to break out in hives. It was like being made into one of the pod people. Who does that?

"It'll be fun."

"It will?"

How had I ended up with someone who thought that would be fun?

See, this is the problem with real, live relationships. The other person has all these weird ticks and traits you never imagined and suddenly you have to make the choice to go along with them (the easy route) or to resist (the awkward one) or to just flat-out run for the hills because if this is what they're letting you see now then who knows what they're hiding under the surface.

I really wanted to run. But he had such gorgeous blue eyes. And he'd pulled a Bridget Jones on me and told me he liked me just the way I was, flaws and all. How could I run from that?

Instead I bowed my head in defeat. "We can go in costumes, but please, keep it within reason? And no Marilynn."

"Hans and Leia?"

"No."

"Ah, darn. I thought you'd look good in a chainmail bikini."

"Matthew Allen Barnes, my grandpa is sitting right here."

My grandpa just chuckled and patted my hand. "It's alright. It's good to see you two together."

He'd campaigned for it pretty much from the day I opened the front door to find Officer Barnes in uniform ready to take my statement on the dead body I'd found up the hill. Of course, he'd known Matt for a lot longer than that. It seems I had, too, since I'd written his name on the wall in permanent marker when I was just a little girl.

I stared at the spot where those letters were still scrawled. Destiny? Maybe. If you believe in that sort of thing.

In a sense the party would be our first outing as a couple, so we really should play it up some. But I was not going to do something like hamburger and fries or two halves of a heart or ketchup and mustard. No, no, no.

CHAPTER 4

Since it was our big send-off party I figured there'd be a pretty good turnout, but I didn't want to leave things to chance, so I paid a visit to Matt's. I wasn't there to see Matt, though. I was there to see one of his current roommates—Sam.

I figured any kid willing to ride his back across the entire valley and offer up every penny in his piggy bank to get help for his mom was a kid with a good dose of chutzpah. And that's exactly what I needed to drum up contestants for the pet parade.

I knocked on the metal screen door of their converted mobile home, listening to the sounds of some shoot 'em up game coming from the living room and took a moment to enjoy the gorgeous view. Matt's place, which he inherited when his dad passed away, wasn't much to look at. Just a brown on brown former mobile home that had been turned into what could pass for a house. But the view behind it was a million-dollar view.

"Come in," Jack shouted.

I stepped inside to find Jack and Sam sprawled on an old brown couch in identical positions of laziness, both slouched down halfway with game controllers in hand. Sam was wearing a baseball cap over his bright red hair, but it did nothing to hide all the freckles on his cheeks. That kid had more freckles than there are stars in the sky.

Jack had the same dark good looks as his brother, but a rogue's casual charm. You just knew looking at him that more than one woman had lost all sense and reason at one flash of that smile. To make it worse, he didn't have his shirt on.

I promptly tried to ignore that fact, but Jack being Jack, consummate conman and eagle-eyed expert on women, just smiled a slow, lazy smile.

"Hey, Maggie. You here to see Matt? Or maybe you waited until he was gone so you and I could have some quality time together..." He wiggled his eyebrows.

"Oh, shut up, Jack." I knew better than to fall for that kind of charm. Ever.

"I know. Matt's the only man for you. You know...I do believe you owe me for that one."

I *was* grateful to him for manipulating me into finally confessing my feelings to Matt, but the thought of owing him a favor made me very nervous. He'd supposedly decided to clean up his act and was doing well so far—especially now that he was responsible for Sam—but I wouldn't put it past him to show up on my front door one night with something body-shaped wrapped in a tarp and ask if I had an extra shovel he could borrow.

"Yeah, well, just keep it reasonable would you? I'm very happy to be with Matt, but I am not going to jail for you Mr. Jackson Barnes."

He guffawed. "Yes, ma'am. Now what brings you by?"

"Actually, I have a business proposal for Sam. You

want a chance to replenish that piggy bank of yours?"

Sam perked up. "Yes."

Jack pushed him gently back. "Now, now. Let's not be too eager. What do you need? What are you willing to pay?"

"Oh it's going to be like that, is it?" I narrowed my eyes at them but couldn't hide my slight smile. (I do not have a poker face. Only reason I win at that game is because I'm so unpredictable seasoned players can't figure out my range.) "Alright. Here's the deal. We're going to have a store closing Halloween party at the barkery. And part of the party is going to be a pet parade. I'm thinking cute dogs in cute costumes. And I thought that if you were to recruit for me I could pay you…fifty cents per entrant."

"Okay." Sam bounced in place.

"Hold up, sport. Not so fast. Fifty cents? That's not enough. Five dollars."

"Per pet? Are you kidding me? We're not even charging anyone to enter. I'll give you a dollar for each one."

"Let me consult with my client." Jack leaned over and whispered to Sam who whispered back with a sly little smile on his face. Great. Instead of Sam helping Jack clean up his act Jack was going to corrupt him.

Jack nodded to Sam. "It's your deal."

Sam sat up looking very serious. "Here are our terms. We'll accept one dollar per pet. But we also want a slice of cake each."

"Hm. I can do that. But every entrant has to be in costume. It's not enough that they show up, they have to be dressed to impress."

Jack smiled. "Oh, don't you worry about that part. It'll be a pet parade you'll never forget."

He was up to something. I just didn't know what. "And keep it legal, please."

"Of course. I am a new and reformed man after all."

He winked as I turned to leave and I shuddered to think what I'd gotten myself into. But at least that was one less task I had to worry about.

I hoped.

CHAPTER 5

At last the big day arrived. I tried not to cry as I pulled the van up at the far edge of the parking lot and looked across at my well-loved but short-lived adventure in running a business. I didn't care what anyone said, I still loved that sign with its hard-to-read cursive script and its cheesy little Newfie heads on either end.

And I'd miss retreating out back at the end of a long day to have a beer with Jamie while the dogs ran around in the fenced area and Fancy made a mad dash for the creek, wallowing in the water like it was a second home.

We hadn't done bad for a first business. Jamie had done particularly well with her cinnamon rolls. And I'd managed a decent online following. But Mason and Greta had seen the real potential. High-end. Flashy. Slick. The type of experience that attracts people who don't bat an eye at a two-hundred-dollar chiropractor appointment for Fifi, their teacup poodle.

It was time to level up.

But first, a party.

When I walked inside, Jamie was in full drill instructor mode, directing a slew of volunteers in setting things up just right. She's the one with style so she was in charge of the decorations and activities. We were using not only the area out back of the barkery but the interior and half of the parking lot, too. It was going to be a madhouse.

Assuming anyone showed. Which I really hoped they did. Sam and Jack had been walking around like cats with a canary so I assumed we'd be okay although some part of me was very, very nervous about why they seemed so smug.

Out back there were all sorts of games for the dogs. Instead of bobbing for apples we had bobbing for balls. And there was a little obstacle course for them to run with a ramp and one of those hollow tubes that Fancy would never ever get near. There was also a game where they had to retrieve the stuffed pumpkin while navigating a minefield of tasty treats.

(Did you ever see that video of the golden retriever that failed the obedience test miserably but had so much fun with all the toys that it was supposed to ignore? I was kind of hoping for that to be honest. Better to have fun than to "win".)

And, of course, there was the costume contest with a grand prize of a Booberry Biscuit crown held together with peanut butter.

Out front was for the human contingent. We had hot cider and hot chocolate for drinks and then fresh cotton candy, caramel corn, and funnel cakes. We'd rented the little carts you see at amusement parks. That was definitely not going to be my role, though. I've made cotton candy before and had the sugared-over hair to prove it. And I wasn't allowed near a funnel cake machine ever since an incident that involved a pair of tongs and hot oil running down the back of my hand.

Inside would be seating for everyone who decided it was a little too chill outside. It was late October in Colorado after all. Honestly, we were incredibly lucky there was no snow on the ground or in the forecast. But that didn't make it warm.

Before I could get too teary about it being our last day of operations, Jamie put me to work. For the next two hours we arranged and cleaned and debated logistics and rearranged until everything looked perfect.

And then it was time to change and get the party started.

CHAPTER 6

I got Fancy into her costume first. It wasn't hard. Just get her into the harness and start up the GoPro. We'd already strapped the fake notepad and pen to the back of it. She wasn't going to win any prizes and she wasn't a panda like I'd wanted, but she actually looked pretty good.

Of course, I'm biased.

Before I could sneak off to Jamie's to put on my costume Matt showed up. After all that debate we'd settled on the couple from *Grease*, so he had his hair slicked back 50's style, with tight jeans, a white t-shirt, and a black leather jacket. It was a good look for him. A very good look.

He was holding something behind his back, but I didn't really care what because I was too busy gawking. I felt another little thrill at the thought that this amazing man was mine, but shook it off.

"It suits you," I said.

"Thanks. Can't wait to see your outfit."

I winced. I'd wanted to do Sandy as she was at the start of the movie—all poodle skirt and ponytail—but Matt had argued for Sexy Sandy in puffed out hair and slim-fitting black outfit. I hadn't let him see it yet, though. I don't know why. Nerves I guess. I have a few more curves than Olivia Newton John ever did. (Not that the outfit looked that bad on me. More just self-conscious silliness that I normally don't feel but did when it came to Matt.)

Anyway.

"Speaking of. I better get over to Jamie's to change." I leaned in to give him a quick kiss on the cheek.

"Wait. I, um, I have something for you."

I tilted my head at the nervousness in his voice. "What?"

He blushed and waved whatever it was in his hand. "I, um. I knew this was kind of a hard day for you with the barkery closing and all and that you'd really wanted Fancy to dress up as a panda and…well…Here."

He shoved one of those brown plastic grocery bags into my hand, the type that are all thin plastic that tears apart at the slightest effort.

"Sorry for the wrapping. I forgot and then I was running late and…"

"That's okay."

I opened it up and had to almost bite my lip to keep from crying. I would've bit my lip if Matt hadn't been watching me.

This is going to sound stupid. I know you won't get it. Who would? I mean, I was thirty-six-years-old for crying out loud.

But what he'd given me was…

Perfect. And sweet. And absolutely adorable.

Somehow, I don't know how, he'd managed to find a stuffed Newfie and then he'd put that Newfie into a panda costume. It was a mini Fancy. In costume.

I wanted to melt. I wanted to go all soft and fuzzy and cry-ey right then and there. But I couldn't. Because to him I was this strong, capable, sarcastic woman and seeing me go all gooey would probably scare him right back into enlisting.

So I just flashed him a smiled instead. "Thank you. It's…I love it. But I better get changed. Don't want to be late."

I fled to the office and took a quick moment to collect myself, staring at that stupid stuffed dog that was so ridiculously perfect for me that it made my heart ache trying very hard not to cry. When I'd finally wrangled my feelings into submission I tucked it away on the top shelf and ran off to Jamie's to get changed, pushing Fancy aside as I snuck away before I could see Matt again.

CHAPTER 7

Of course, I couldn't hide how emotional I was from Jamie. And I didn't need to either. She was my best friend. She knew when something absolutely wrecked me. So we bounced around her living room like teenagers as I told her what Matt had done.

I don't know how to describe to you why that hit me so deep. Maybe because it showed that he really got me? I mean it was a stuffed animal. Who gives a grown woman a stuffed animal? But it was perfect *for me.* Because it was about Fancy and about her dressing up as a panda and it was because the barkery was closing and he'd remembered and he got that this was a big day for me even though I was supposedly moving on to something bigger and better with the pet resort.

And…

I know. All this silly relationship stuff, right?

I'll stop now, I promise. It's perfectly normal to have a boyfriend. And for that boyfriend to give you caring gifts. And from here on out I will pretend that was perfectly normal for me, too—that I wasn't some spinster-bound misanthrope who was insanely lucky to have found a man who was actually worth my time.

So anyway. Great, caring gift. Whatever.

Time to get dressed.

I slipped into a ridiculously fitted pair of black slacks and off-the-shoulder black top and then added red heels that were going to break my ankle before the end of the day. Then to top it all off I let Jamie destroy my hair in a way I hope to never repeat again. I'm pretty sure she used an entire can of hairspray. I have no doubt that had anyone come within five feet of me with a match I would've gone up like a torch.

That's what dressing up for Halloween will get you.

I still didn't know what she was going as until she ducked into her room and came back out with her hair in pigtails tied with ribbon, a cutesy blue dress, a basket with a fake little dog in it, and ruby red slippers.

"Dorothy from the Wizard of Oz?"

She nodded. "Lulu is going to be the lion and Mason is going to be the scarecrow."

"Tell me that involves wearing bib overalls."

"And a plaid shirt."

I clapped my hands together. "And is Lulu going to have one of those lion ruffs like on that commercial with the baby?"

"Yes. She looks so cute. I can't wait until you see it. Mason's bringing her. I figured otherwise she'd run herself ragged before things even got started."

"Makes sense. Fancy was definitely ready for a nap when I headed over here. Then again, Fancy is always ready for a nap."

We stood side-by-side in front of her mirror. It was an interesting contrast. Me in my skin-tight outfit and ratted out hair and her in her pigtails and bobby socks.

She pulled out her camera. "Here. Selfie time. And then we have to get back before things fall apart."

"Tell me about it. I can't believe I left Jack in charge of registration for the pet parade."

"Neither can I." We leaned our heads together and she took the photo. She showed it to me. "What do you think?"

I laughed. "I think that's us to a T. Opposites that are somehow complements."

I took a deep breath. "I'm scared, Jamie. Things are changing so fast and..."

She squeezed my arm. "It's going to be okay, Maggie. You'll see. Now come on. We have a costume contest to judge."

CHAPTER 8

I had to deal with the usual complement of hubba-hubbas and wolf whistles from Jack when Jamie and I made it back to the barkery. It's quite possible I said a few things to him my grandma wouldn't want to hear, but he deserved every single one.

He wouldn't let us see the contestants before the parade. Claimed that it would bias our judging. Instead he led us to a raised platform off to the side of the little parade path that wound its way through the parking lot.

There were maybe a hundred people gathered to see the "parade", but a lot of familiar faces were missing, so I assumed they were signed up to participate.

I looked towards the end of the lot where the parade was going to start, but I couldn't see anything past the very large vehicles that were parked there. I counted at least three horse trailers. And one cattle trailer?

I looked back at Jack. "What did you do?"

He grinned. "You said it was a pet parade. And that they had to be in costume. Those were the only rules you gave us."

"Pets, Jack. Pets. Like dogs and cats."

Jamie caught my look of concern. "What? What is it?"

I glanced towards the end of the parking lot one last time before sitting down with a huff. I knew I should go investigate but already I hated my red high heels enough that I wanted to torch them when I was done. "I think we're about to watch a very interesting pet parade…" I glared at Jack. "This goes wrong, it's on you Jackson Barnes."

"Don't worry. Matt wouldn't let me do anything too drastic. It's why you don't have an elephant in a tutu in the mix although I'm sure Tootsie would've won the grand prize."

He winked at me and left to get things started.

I wanted to believe he was joking, but I was pretty sure he wasn't.

❀ ❀ ❀

The parade started out relatively normal. First in line was Greta with her Irish Wolfhound, Hans. He's such a dignified old soul I was surprised to see him in any costume at all. Then again, he's infernally well-behaved, so he was also capable of pulling off any costume. (Unlike Fancy. Who I love. Dearly. I swear.)

Greta had dressed him like a king with a deep purple cape and a crown and a little scepter sewn to the front of the cape.

He carried it off like a champ. She'd set aside her customary black slacks and bright tops for a matching ball gown that looked like it was actually real, right down to the delicate tiara resting on her pale blond hair.

Right behind them was Mason with Lulu. Not only was he wearing ratty old bib overalls and a flannel shirt with straw poking out of it but he also had on scuffed up boots that looked like they were a hundred years old. It was great.

And Lulu made for an adorable lion. She was a little excited by the crowd and didn't want to walk along the actual parade path, especially when she saw Jamie up on the podium, but she did really well for a puppy.

Behind them came Evan and Abe and their Saint Bernard, Lucy Carrots. All three were dressed as pirates. Abe even had a fake parrot on his shoulder. How he'd managed to get Lucy to wear her pirate's hat I do not know, but she did.

By that point I was already overwhelmed with adorableness.

But the next contestant in line had me almost choking on my Coke. It was Sam and Jack walking along with a miniature horse. Not a dog dressed like a horse. Oh no. It was an actual horse.

And she was dressed like a hippie with a little peace symbol headband running across her forehead and flowers braided into her mane. Her little feet even had beaded fringe that jingled when she walked.

Sam ran over to me, grinning ear to ear. "That's Lady. Isn't she great? We didn't have a dog to bring. Although I want one and Jack said maybe we can get one but not now. Maybe later. Maybe a big one like you have. But in the meantime he said we could bring Lady. She's Jack's new boss's best friend's horse. He normally uses her for kids' parties, but we were able to borrow her for today. And isn't she just the greatest? Now I think I want a horse instead. Can we get a horse, Jack?" he called.

Jack just smiled. "Maybe, champ. We'll talk about it more later."

"She's going to win. I just know she is." Sam ran back to Lady who continued to plod along, her warm brown eyes full of endless patience and a surprising amount of intelligence.

The next few were more normal.

James, the fishing guide, had dressed his dog up as a trout. (It didn't work very well.)

Dean, manager of the conference center and resort, brought a Chihuahua dressed as a monkey. (That one was pretty clever.)

Russell surprised all of us by dressing his old hunting dog up as a peacock. (Very bright if nothing else.)

And Darryl the hunting guide dressed his dog up as a pumpkin. (He got points for effort if nothing else.)

Fancy made her appearance, too, with Matt leading her along the parade route through the surreptitious use of a never-stopping supply of treats in his left hand. I was pretty sure most of the video footage we were going to get of the event would just be of Fancy eating something, but that was okay.

Next came a handful of cats in various costumes. A lion, as you might expect. (Although not near as cute as Lulu.) An Ewok. (*That* was beyond cute.) And a sunflower and a dinosaur and a few others I'm sure I've forgotten.

And then things got interesting again.

There was a llama dressed as a loofa. And a cow dressed as a hippo that didn't really want to move and never actually made it off the starting line. And three goats in bow ties, one of whom tried to eat a funnel cake, plate and all, that some little kid held too close to him.

And last, but not least, an emu dressed as a football player which was not the least bit happy about it.

"Jack! Your problem, fix it," I shouted when the emu started to fight its trainer and the crowd realized that maybe they wanted to be somewhere not so close to a big angry bird.

Fortunately, Matt jumped in, too, and between the three of them they got the emu back in its cage.

It was quite the assortment. And a miracle that they all seemed to behave themselves more or less. I had planned to get a big group picture of all of the contestants, but realized that was just not going to happen if I wanted to avoid an actual incident.

At least everyone had seemed to enjoy it.

CHAPTER 9

Jamie and I decided we needed one more pass through the contestants before we chose our winners. There was a lot of cuteness involved and it deserved some serious consideration. Plus, I just wanted to pet the dogs. And Lady.

I ran into Greta first. She was studying the chaos as one of the goats—probably the same one who'd gone after the funnel cake—chomped away on the llama's loofa costume and the cow adamantly refused to return to its trailer.

"This was fun, yes? I think we will do this again next year at the resort. Jack has promised me an elephant in a tutu."

I laughed. "It was fun. But maybe we skip the elephant."

Greta shrugged one shoulder and I knew that I better start planning for an elephant in a tutu at next year's parade.

I made my way to where Fancy had plopped down on her side in the shade. She looked thoroughly done with the whole thing. Lady stood next to her chewing on some grass she'd snuck from the side of the parking lot.

Matt stood between them, arms crossed.

I stepped closer. "Well done with leading Fancy. I told you she'll do pretty much anything for a treat."

"Yep. Here." Matt shoved Fancy's leash and Lady's reins into my hands and strode away.

I watched him go, baffled. What had I said?

He joined in with the group wrangling the cow into its trailer and I relaxed some. So it wasn't about me. It was just he wanted to help out. But then he kept going, helping get all of the animals back in their pens or cages. Finally, he returned.

I tried again. "Quite the parade. I knew your brother was up to something, I just didn't know what."

I smiled at him but he didn't smile back. "You okay?" I asked.

"Yeah. Fine. Here. I've got Fancy if you want to go back and announce the winners."

"Matt?" He hadn't even said something about my costume and he wouldn't meet my eyes. "What's wrong?"

"Nothing."

Before I could push him further Jamie came over. "We better announce the winners so everyone can get out of here."

"Right." I glanced back at Matt as we returned to the judging platform. He was watching me, but the look in his eyes was most definitely not happy.

Relationships suck. Seriously. How does anyone navigate their way through one?

But I put that all aside as I stood on the platform. "Sam, come here." I motioned for him to join us.

He ran up the steps, cheeks pink with excitement.

"Ladies and Gentlemen, you have Sam here to thank

for the wide variety of participants in today's pet parade, so I'm going to let him announce your winners."

I handed him the microphone and whispered in his ear what to say.

He stumbled a few times in that breathless way kids have, but he managed. "The judges have chosen three winners. One dog, one cat, and one other. The dog winner is…"

Jack made a fake drumroll noise for him.

"Lucy Carrots as a Pirate of the Carrot-be-an." (That would be pronounced like Caribbean but with carrot in there instead. Yeah, it threw me, too.)

Abe and Evan led Lucy on to the stage where Jamie handed them the Booberry Biscuit crown. They swapped it out for her pirate hat but she promptly shook it off her head and devoured it, leaving a big puddle of crumbs and drool in her wake.

"The second winner is The Amazing Miss Maisy as an Ewok."

That was the cat. She was given a small bowl of cream which she delicately lapped up as her owner watched in pride.

"And the last winner," Sam jumped in place when I told him, "is Lady as a Groovy Granny." He ran over to Lady, still holding the microphone, and gave her a great big hug around the neck. Lady for her part just stood there until Sam showed her the apple she'd won. That she took and delicately chomped to pieces.

"And that concludes our pet parade," I shouted. "Thank you everyone and please enjoy the food and drinks."

I turned away, wanting desperately to cry now that it

was really over, but forcing myself to walk down the steps of the platform and mingle with the remaining guests.

I tried to remind myself that this wasn't the end of everything. It was just the end of a chapter, that's all. But it was hard to make myself actually believe it.

CHAPTER 10

After the party we gathered all of our volunteers and friends inside for red chili, cornbread, and a viewing of the Fancy parade footage.

I quickly changed out of that ridiculous outfit and put on shoes worth walking in, but the hair was going to take at least a shower or two to get back to normal.

I stood by the counter with Jamie as everyone talked and laughed and ate. It was a good feeling to see all those people who were a part of our lives gathered together.

"We didn't do that bad with this place, did we?" I asked.

"No. We didn't." She hip-checked me. "We would've made it work, Maggie. You know we would've."

"Only because of your cinnamon rolls."

She laughed. "No. Because you'd never let us fail."

"Neither would you."

"Exactly."

I crossed my arms and studied Matt who'd managed to wedge himself in a corner with Jack on one side and Sam on the other.

"Matt's mad at me."

"What for?"

"I honestly don't know."

"Well, make him tell you. You guys are good together, Maggie. But no relationship is perfect. You're going to have bumps along the way."

I raised an eyebrow. "Oh really. I haven't seen you and Mason have any bumps."

"Oh we have them, believe me. You know he wants to invite five hundred people to our wedding? And have it at the country club?"

I shuddered. "That sounds like my idea of a horror movie."

Jamie laughed. "Well, when you find someone you love, you make those kinds of sacrifices for them. Go on. Don't let this fester. Find out what's wrong."

I made my way over to their table with four slices of cake on a tray.

"Well, Sam, it wasn't what I expected, but you certainly delivered on the deal we made. Here you go. Twenty-five dollars and two slices of cake."

"Twenty-five? But we only…"

Jack shushed him. "Thank you very much. Pleasure doing business with you."

I shook my head. "Jack, I swear if you corrupt this boy…there will be hell to pay."

"Yes, ma'am. Come on, Sam. You can eat your cake while I get the Fancy footage going."

He led Sam to the barkery counter where we'd placed a television, and started working on hooking up the GoPro from Fancy. I didn't expect it would show anything useful, but hopefully it would be entertaining.

I sat down next to Matt. "Are you going to tell me what's wrong?"

"Nothing's wrong."

I might have said a word I won't repeat here that said he was lying. "I can't fix something if you won't tell me about it, Matt."

"Nothing's wrong. I think I'll go help Jack."

"Fine. I think I will too."

He glared at me, but what could he do? It was my store and my television and my video footage.

Just as we reached Jack, the video started to play. And it was completely focused on me. I'd never realized until that moment how much Fancy followed me around or watched me.

A room full of people and I was her world.

"Awww, look at that." I glanced towards where Fancy was sleeping in her cubby. "You silly goof."

On screen Matt walked up to me, the brown plastic bag tucked behind his back.

Next to me Matt tensed. "You can fast forward through this. No one wants to see it."

"I do," I snapped, giving Jack a glare as he reached towards the fast forward button.

Somehow Fancy had been positioned perfectly to capture the entire moment. So I saw the shy pride on Matt's face when I pulled the stuffed animal out of the bag and smiled.

And then the way his face crumpled when I turned away from him so abruptly afterward and hurried away.

I was going to say something to him. Apologize. Try to explain.

But the footage on the screen continued as Fancy followed me into the office and I stood there, wiping away a tear and pulling myself together before kissing the stuffed animal on the nose and tucking it away on the top shelf.

"No one will mess with it there, will they, Fancy?" I said on screen with one last sniff, clearly overcome with emotion.

"So you didn't hate it," Matt whispered.

"Of course I didn't. It was perfect." I turned away, trying not to cry again, but Matt spun me around and pulled me close.

I buried my face against his chest and then looked into those oh-so-blue eyes of his. "I'm sorry. I didn't want you to see me blubber. I thought you might run for the hills if you did."

He kissed the tip of my nose. "You can blubber all you want. I'll still love you."

I stopped breathing. It was the first time he'd used the L word for real. I didn't know how I was supposed to respond.

On screen a dog barked and right behind us Fancy jumped to her feet, barking, which set off Lulu and Lucy Carrots.

By the time we got them all calmed back down the moment had passed.

I turned back to Matt. "So we're okay?"

He nodded. "We are."

I rubbed the back of my neck. "You should know I suck at this. At relationships. But, I do love you, alright?"

He laughed and pulled me in for a kiss. "Alright."

We spent the rest of the night surrounded by family and friends watching Fancy's view of the most bizarre pet parade I'd ever seen.

It was a good night. A really good one. A bootastic one, if I do say so myself.

🐾 🐾 🐾

If you haven't yet read them and you want to spend more time with Maggie, Fancy, and the crew, the mystery that follows the events in this short story, is ***A Sabotaged Celebration and Salmon Snaps*** *or you can start at the beginning with* ***A Dead Man and Doggie Delights.***

ABOUT THE AUTHOR

When Aleksa Baxter decided to write what she loves it was a no-brainer to write a cozy mystery set in the mountains of Colorado where she grew up and starring a Newfie, Miss Fancypants, that is very much like her own Newfie, in both the good ways and the bad.

🐾 🐾 🐾

You can reach her at aleksabaxterwriter@gmail.com or on her website aleksabaxter.com.

www.ingramcontent.com/pod-product-compliance
Lightning Source LLC
Chambersburg PA
CBHW070454170726
48291CB00005B/1751

* 9 7 8 1 9 5 0 9 0 2 6 4 4 *